# THE EMPEROR'S NEW CLOTHES

**Dona Herweck Rice**

**Editorial Director**
Dona Herweck Rice

**Assistant Editors**
Leslie Huber, M.A.
Katie Das

**Editor-in-Chief**
Sharon Coan, M.S.Ed.

**Editorial Manager**
Gisela Lee, M.A.

**Creative Director**
Lee Aucoin

**Illustration Manager/Designer**
Timothy J. Bradley

**Illustrator**
Chad Thompson

**Publisher**
Rachelle Cracchiolo, M.S.Ed.

**Teacher Created Materials**
*5301 Oceanus Drive*
*Huntington Beach, CA 92649-1030*
**http://www.tcmpub.com**
**ISBN 978-1-4333-0167-4**
*© 2008 by Teacher Created Materials, Inc.*

# The Emperor's New Clothes

## Story Summary

There is an empire ruled by a vain and silly emperor. People in the empire tell the emperor what he wants to hear. They flatter him. They say he is handsome and wise.

One day, two tailors come to town. They promise to make the emperor the best clothes ever seen. They will weave the fabric themselves. The tailors say that only smart people who are fit for their jobs can see the clothes.

The emperor pays the tailors many bags of gold to make the clothes. The problem is that the emperor can not see the clothes! No one else can see them either. But the people do not say anything. They do not want to be called stupid and lose their jobs!

The truth is that the tailors do not make any clothes at all. They just pretend to make them. They trick the emperor and take the gold. But there is one honest child in the town. Will the child tell the emperor the truth? Read the story to find out.

# Tips for Performing Reader's Theater

## Adapted from Aaron Shepard

- Don't let your script hide your face. If you can't see the audience, your script is too high.

- Look up often when you speak. Don't just look at your script.

- Talk slowly so the audience knows what you are saying.

- Talk loudly so everyone can hear you.

- Talk with feelings. If the character is sad, let your voice be sad. If the character is surprised, let your voice be surprised.

- Stand up straight. Keep your hands and feet still.

- Remember that even when you are not talking, you are still your character.

- Narrator, be sure to give the characters enough time for their lines.

# Tips for Performing
# Reader's Theater *(cont.)*

- If the audience laughs, wait for them to stop before you speak again.

- If someone in the audience talks, don't pay attention.

- If someone walks into the room, don't pay attention.

- If you make a mistake, pretend it was right.

- If you drop something, try to leave it where it is until the audience is looking somewhere else.

- If the reader forgets to read his or her part, see if you can read the part instead, make something up, or just skip over it.  Don't whisper to the reader!

- If a reader falls down during the performance, pretend it didn't happen.

# The Emperor's New Clothes

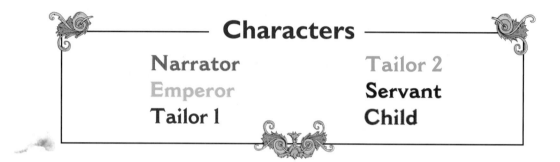

## Characters

| | |
|---|---|
| Narrator | Tailor 2 |
| Emperor | Servant |
| Tailor 1 | Child |

## Setting

This reader's theater takes place in a town. The town is in the middle of an empire. A vain emperor rules the empire.

# Act 1

| | |
|---|---|
| **Narrator:** | Two tailors sit by the side of a road. The road leads into a town. There is a palace in the town. |
| **Tailor 1:** | We need to make some money. It is time to get to work. |
| **Tailor 2:** | Work? You want to work? |
| **Tailor 1:** | I want to do what we do best. You know what I mean. |
| **Tailor 2:** | Oh, yes! Let's get to work! |
| **Narrator:** | Just then, a child passes by. |

**Tailor 1:** Who lives in the palace, child?

**Child:** The emperor lives there.

**Tailor 2:** Is he a smart man?

**Child:** No, he is not. He is handsome, though. He likes to look in the mirror.

**Narrator:** The tailors smile at each other. They wave to the child. Then they walk to the palace.


**Poem: Old King Cole**


**Emperor:** Just look at me, will you? Have you ever seen a more handsome man? I could look at myself all day!

**Servant:** Yes, sire. You are handsome. I am lucky to serve you.

**Emperor:** That is true!

**Servant:** Can I get more mirrors for you?

**Emperor:** No. These ten will do.

**Servant:** I think I hear a knock at the door. May I leave you to answer it?

**Emperor:** Yes, but be quick. You will be sad to be far from me.

**Narrator:** The servant bows and goes to the door. He opens it.

**Servant:** May I help you?

**Tailor 1:** We are here to help *you*!

**Tailor 2:** You will be happy to know what we can do.

**Servant:** What can you do?

**Tailor 1:** Take us to the emperor. He will want to hear all about it.

**Servant:** Why should I?

**Tailor 2:** The emperor will love what we can do. He will praise you for taking us to him.

**Servant:** Oh, I see. Well, then, come this way.

**Narrator:** The servant takes the tailors to the emperor. The emperor is looking at himself in all ten mirrors.

**Emperor:**    Oh, what a handsome man!

**Servant:**    So handsome!

**Tailor 1:**    Oh, yes, sire!

**Tailor 2:**    There is no one more handsome than you!

**Emperor:**    True.  But who are you?

**Tailor 1:**    We are tailors.

**Tailor 2:**    We have come here to help you.

**Tailor 1:**    We have heard how handsome you are.

**Tailor 2:**    And we know how to make clothes for a very handsome man.

**Tailor 1:**   No one else has these clothes.

Tailor 2:   You will have the only set.

Emperor:   Tell me more!

**Tailor 1:**   We will weave fabric from special thread. It will be the best fabric ever. It will be almost as handsome as you!

Tailor 2:   Here is the best part. Only smart people who are fit for their jobs can see the fabric. You will know who is stupid. Then you can get rid of them.

Emperor:   I must have these clothes! Make them at once! Servant, bring the tailors all the gold they need. Take them to the sewing room.

**Servant:**     Yes, sire!

Tailor 1:     We will begin at once.

# Act 2

Narrator:     The tailors work in the sewing room for days. They ask for fine food. They ask for gold and silver thread.

**Child:**     Those tailors work hard. I see a light in the window each night. The clothes must be great.

### Song: Pop! Goes the Weasel

Emperor:     Servant, I want to know what the clothes look like. Go to the sewing room to see them. Then come tell me about them.

**Servant:**     Yes, sire.

**Narrator:**     The servant knocks on the door.

**Tailor 1:**     Come in!

**Tailor 2:**     You must be here to see the clothes. They are not done yet.  But you can see the fabric.

**Tailor 1:**     Yes.  Come and feel it, too.

**Servant:**     Okay.  But where is it?

**Tailor 2:**     Right here, of course.

**Narrator:**     The servant does not see anything.

**Servant:**     Oh, yes, I see.  It is very soft.

**Narrator:** The servant lies.

**Servant:** I must be going. I will tell the emperor what I saw.

**Narrator:** The servant leaves the room.

**Servant:** Oh, no! What can I do? I must not be fit for my job. I did not see anything!

**Narrator:** The servant goes back to the emperor.

**Emperor:** Well, what did you see?

**Servant:** I saw such handsome fabric! It is soft, too. You will look great.

**Emperor:** Of course I will. I am always handsome.

**Servant:** Yes, sire.

**Narrator:** The servant lets out a big sigh.

**Emperor:** Servant, I want you to plan a parade. I will wear the new clothes. Then everyone can see how handsome I am.

**Servant:** Yes, sire. As you wish.

# Act 3

**Tailor 1:** It is time to show our work.

**Tailor 2:** I love this part!

**Narrator:** The tailors hold out their arms. They pretend to carry clothes on them. They take the clothes to the emperor.

**Tailor 1:** Sire, we have your clothes.

**Tailor 2:** We do hope you like them.

**Emperor:** Well, where are they?

**Tailor 1:** They are right here, sire.

**Tailor 2:** May I help you put them on?

**Emperor:** Oh, yes. Please do. They are very nice clothes.

| | |
|---|---|
| **Narrator:** | The emperor lies. He can not see the clothes! He wonders if he is fit for his job. He wants everyone to think so. |
| **Emperor:** | Oh, look at me! I am so handsome. |
| **Narrator:** | But the emperor is really only wearing his underwear. |
| **Tailor 1:** | So handsome! |
| **Tailor 2:** | Perfect! |
| **Servant:** | It is time for the parade, sire. |
| **Narrator:** | The emperor does not want people to see him in his underwear. But he does not know what else to do. He does not want people to think he is stupid! He goes out to the parade. |

| | |
|---|---|
| **Tailor 1,** Tailor 2, **and Servant:** | Hurrah! |
| **Child:** | What is he doing? |
| **Servant:** | He is showing us his new clothes. |
| **Child:** | What do you mean? |
| **Tailor 1:** | Hush, child! |
| Tailor 2: | The emperor will hear you. |
| **Child:** | So what?  Does he know what he is doing? |
| **Servant:** | What do you mean? |

**Child:**      He is not wearing any clothes!

**Servant:**      What?

Emperor:      What?

**Child:**      The emperor is not wearing any clothes!

Narrator:      The tailors look at each other.

**Tailor 1:**      We had better get out of here.

Tailor 2:      Let's go!

**Child:**      Stop those tailors! They lied. They did not make any clothes.

Emperor:      Oh, no! Bring me a robe!

**Child:** Do not be silly. Who cares how you look? It is better to be wise.

**Emperor:** You are right, child. Thank you for telling me the truth. I want to give you a job. You will be my royal truth teller. You are the only brave one here.

**Child:** Okay. I will take the job. But be sure. I will always tell the truth!

**Emperor:** That is good.

**Child:** I will start now. It is time to get rid of your mirrors!

**Narrator:** The emperor smiles. He knows that the child is right.

# Old King Cole
## Traditional

Old King Cole was a merry old soul,
And a merry old soul was he.
He called for his pipe, and he called for his bowl,
And he called for his fiddlers three.

Every fiddler he had a fiddle,
And a very fine fiddle had he.
Oh, there's none so rare, as can compare
With King Cole and his fiddlers three.

# Pop! Goes the Weasel

## Traditional

All around the cobbler's bench
The monkey chased the weasel.
The monkey thought 'twas all in fun.
Pop! goes the weasel.

A penny for a spool of thread,
A penny for a needle;
That's the way the money goes.
Pop! goes the weasel.

For you may try to sew and sew,
But you'll never make anything regal.
That's the way the money goes.
Pop! goes the weasel.

I've no time to plead and pine,
I've no time to wheedle.
Kiss me quick and then I'm gone.
Pop! goes the weasel.

# Glossary

**cobbler's bench**—a shoemaker's work table

**emperor**—a ruler of an empire

**empire**—a kingdom

**fabric**—material used to make clothes and other things

**fit**—good enough for; able to do

**flatter**—to praise to make a person feel good

**loom**—a machine used to weave thread in order to make fabric

**pine**—to wish for with longing

**plead**—to beg

**regal**—for a royal ruler, such as an emperor

**sire**—an important leader, such as an emperor

**spool**—a small tube used to hold thread for sewing

**tailor**—a person who makes and mends clothes

**vain**—very concerned about how one looks

**weave**—to make fabric on a loom with thread

**wheedle**—to beg in a nagging way